Title

Title of Work: The Pumpkin That Hated Halloween

Completion/ Publication

Year of Completion: 2010

Author

Author: Wayne Small, dba Explore Imagination

Author Created: Text

Work made for hire: No

Citizen of: United States

Copyright Claimant

Copyright Claimant: Wayne Small

447 Putnam ave, Brooklyn. NY.11221

Rights and Permissions

Organization Name: Explore Imagination

Email: exploreimagination.com

Address: 447 Putnam ave

Brooklyn, NY United States

Certification

Name: Wayne Small

Date: October 20,2010

Imagine that all you know and fear,
and all the things that haunt and scare,
suddenly at once all appeared.
Well you can find this place once a year.

When the norms only come out in
the light,
and lock their doors before it turns
night,
the entire world is left in a fright,
for the scariest creatures come out
at night.

Children play a game of deceit,
where they dare to ask trick or treat.

Where the guys and gals dress up like ghouls,
to shock and scare the unknowing fools.

Do not be so quick to believe
for the purpose of tonight is to
deceive.
All may enter, but none may leave
on this day we call All Hallows Eve.

In the place known as pumpkin world,
there lived little pumpkin boys and
pumpkin girls,
where each and every pumpkin had its
own name
and different faces, so none were the
same.

The pumpkins were so different from one another
and it wasn't always because of weight, shape, size or color.

Some pumpkins were round, and some pumpkins were square.
Some pumpkins were bald, and some pumpkins had hair.

Some pumpkins had pretty baby faces that made you say
gu-gu, ga-ga, and some had wrinkled old faces like grandma
and grand pa.

Some pumpkins were huge, and others were so little.
Some would make you scream, and others would make you giggle.

Some pumpkins were chubby and others were skinny.
What I'm trying to tell you is that there were just so many.

The pumpkins even walked and dressed in their very own clothes,
and how they walked without feet, only a pumpkin knows.

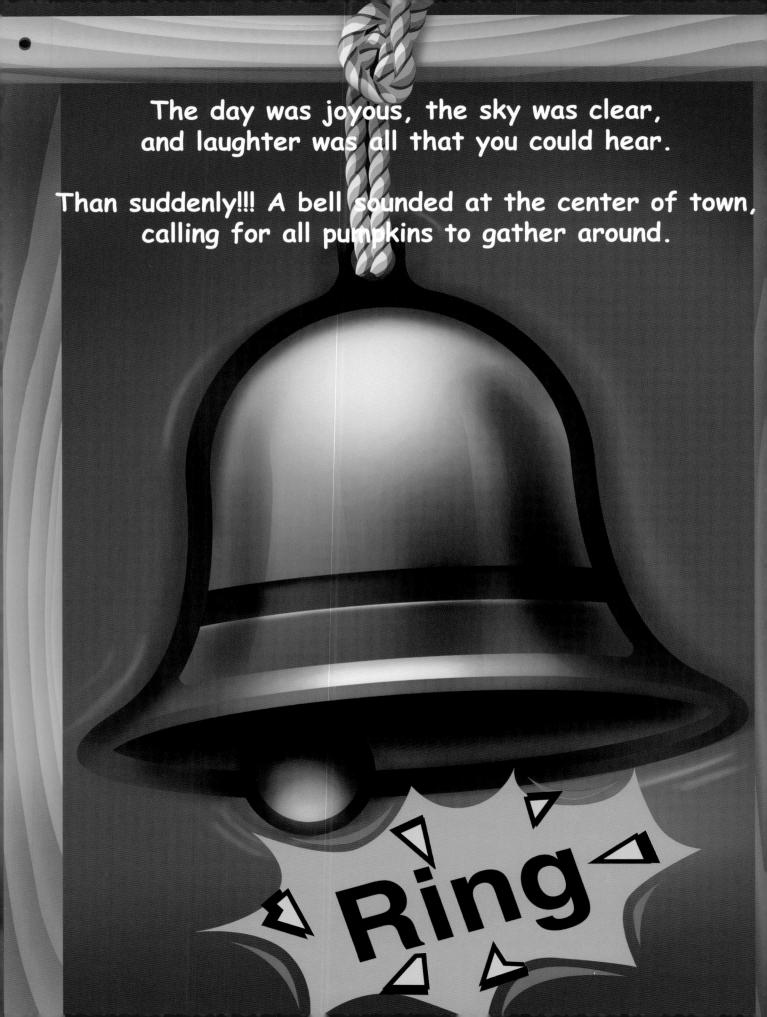

Pumpkins orange and pumpkins purple
all flocked to the pumpkin circle.

It seemed the king of previous years
had asked the pumpkins to lend him their ears.

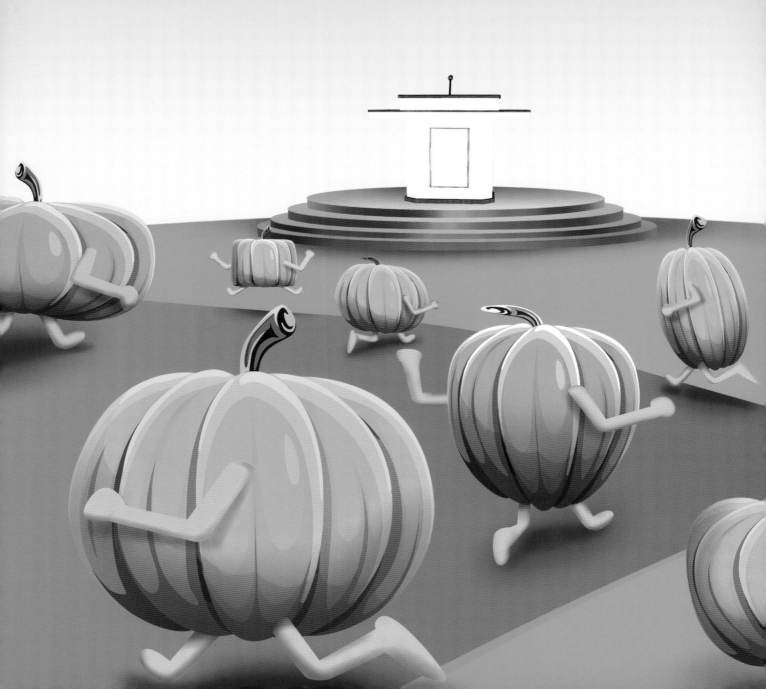

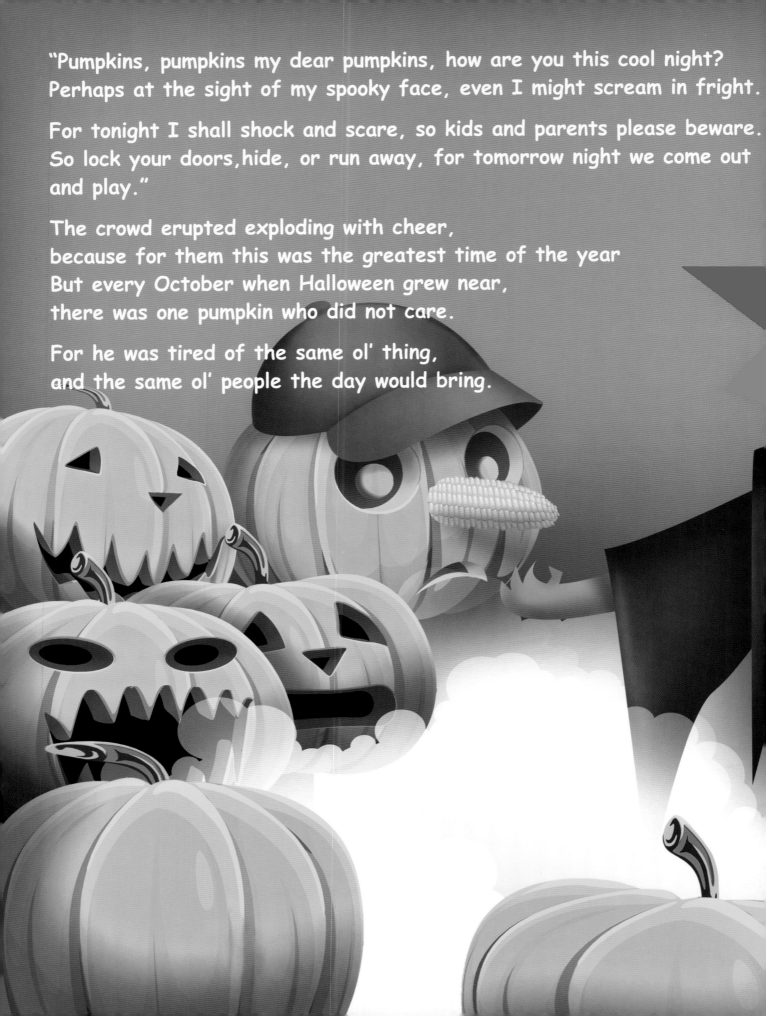

"Pumpkins, pumpkins my dear pumpkins, how are you this cool night?
Perhaps at the sight of my spooky face, even I might scream in fright.

For tonight I shall shock and scare, so kids and parents please beware.
So lock your doors,hide, or run away, for tomorrow night we come out and play."

The crowd erupted exploding with cheer,
because for them this was the greatest time of the year
But every October when Halloween grew near,
there was one pumpkin who did not care.

For he was tired of the same ol' thing,
and the same ol' people the day would bring.

"Halloween, Halloween, I'm sick of Halloween.
I'm sick of seeing things that I have already seen.

Like monsters, goblins, ghouls and ghost,
the costumes are the part that I dislike the most.

Of all the holidays throughout the year,
why is this the only one that we fear?

And another thing I always wanted to ask,
why do we cover up our beautiful faces and put on masks?

It is the stuff of nightmares, the food of dreams
but instead of laughter I only hear screams."

Just once he wished that Halloween wouldn't come.
If only there was a way for it to be done.

So he thought and he thought how to
make a day disappear, and soon the
thought was crystal clear.

So he waited and waited until the end
of the day, and upon a shooting star he
wished Halloween away.

So he went to sleep as he would always do and woke up to a sky that was baby blue.

Then he hopped out of the bed with a very loud scream, WHAT DAY IS IT, WHAT DAY IS IT!!!!!!
And a saddened tone replied, "It's the day after Halloween."

Jack was so happy that his wish had come true, but for what he was in store for he truly had no clue.

So he walked into town where the pumpkins would gather, but instead of feeling joy, he simply felt sadder.

There were no drawings, no mask, nor joy on their faces, no costumes from across the world that made you think of different places.

There was no crowding in the streets, no noise, no music.

There were drums and trumpets but no band to use it.

No decorations, no paintings, no statues were made, no dancing in the streets, no singing, no parades.

No goblins or wizards with long black hats, no crossing paths with bad-luck black cats.

No scary witches on flying brooms, no howling wolves, no bright full moon.

It was exactly what he wished for, but the feeling wasn't right.

It was exactly as he pictured, but he was not pleased with the sight.

Because there was a pain that was so big in his chest, and just emptiness he felt where his heart would rest.

For there was something different something not quite the same, and he knew exactly the pumpkin to blame.

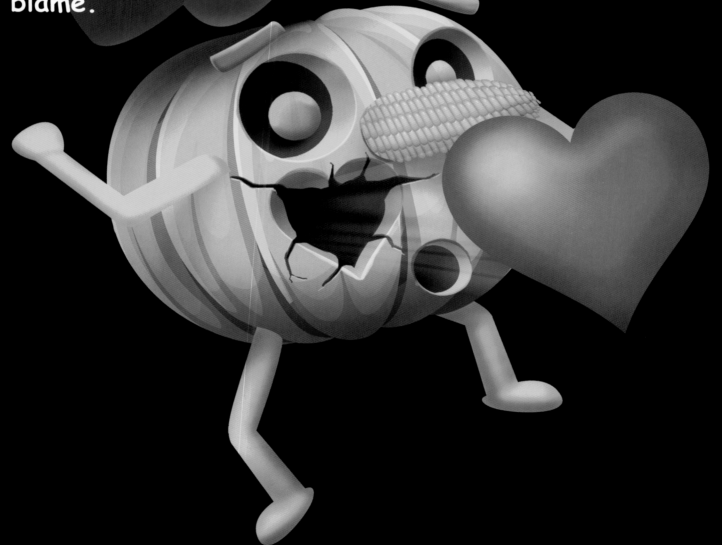

It wasn't as he expected. It was unlike anything he has seen, but now he realized how much Halloween means.

It wasn't about collecting candy from where someone lives. It was that some people were willing to give.

It wasn't about your costume or knowing someone's name. It was that for this one day everyone was the same.

It wasn't about who you were or what people see. It was that you could be anything you wanted to be.

Luckily for Jack things were not the
way they seemed.
The events from today were just things
that he dreamed.
He awoke with a smile that could only
be worn by a child.
As he dashed into the nearby streets,
with thoughts of things he laughed and
sang with dreams of being Halloweens
next king.

HALLOWEEN

Sometimes in the search to find something more, we lose the things we have and cannot return them to the way they were before, so when we wish, we must be sure of the things that we wish, we wish for!

We inspire to become inspired, we awake to experience the dream. Writing is the international passport that will take you to places you have never been. Speech is the power to move without the bodily strength to do so. Imagination is the photo to things that you have never seen. With this philosophy I encourage each child to dream, I challenge each creative mind to explore, I dare every artist to go further than imagining.

For that which is thought to be impossible... It's simple it must be unimaginable...
Wayne Small